Disney's
THE NEW ADVENTURES OF
WINNIE the POOH
Fast Friends

TWIN BOOKS

MALLARD PRESS

Winnie the Pooh was, without a doubt, the slowest bear in the world. He was always late for something.

One day there was a fire drill in the Hundred-Acre Wood, and it was Piglet's turn to jump into the firemen's net. Rabbit held up one end of the net. Pooh was supposed to hold up the other, but as usual, he was late. Pooh walked up just as Piglet bounced off the net. The flying Piglet crashed into Pooh, and they both tumbled to the ground.

Pooh's friends were very angry.

"You can't go around being late all the time," sputtered Gopher. "It throws everything out of whack!"

"Well," said Pooh, feeling sorry, "is there anything I can do to put things back...in whack?"

Rabbit wagged his finger at Pooh. "You could try being on time for once!" he snapped.

Gopher paced back and forth, trying to think of a solution. Then it came to him. "We'll ssspeed the bear up!" said Gopher, grinning. "We'll get him moving like the wind itssself!"

Rabbit tapped his foot impatiently, wondering when all this speeding up was going to happen.

"We're starting now!" said Gopher. And he grabbed Pooh by the arm and led him away.

An hour later, on a nearby hilltop, Gopher introduced the new Pooh. He was dressed in pillows, football helmet, and roller skates. Tigger and Rabbit looked on.

"How's a new wardrobe going to speed him up?" asked Tigger.

"You'll see," said Gopher, nudging Pooh to the edge of the hill. Then, very casually, Gopher gave the bear a shove. Pooh went zooming down the hill.

"Oh, botherrrrrrr!" screamed Pooh.

"You did it!" cried Tigger.

"I never thought I'd see the day he moved like that!" added Rabbit, smiling.

Winnie the Pooh whipped through the Hundred-Acre Wood at blinding speed. He stirred up a wind that ripped leaves from the trees.

"Oh, d-dear," said Piglet as Pooh zipped past him.

Later, Piglet was watching Rabbit work in his garden. "Do you think Pooh's being so very fast is really such a very good thing?" he asked Rabbit.

"It's wonderful!" said Rabbit happily.

But just as he was speaking, Pooh tore through the garden like lightning. The wind in his wake pulled Rabbit's carrots right out of the ground.

"No!" cried Rabbit. But there was nothing he could do. His garden was ruined.

Rabbit and Piglet went to warn Tigger about the new, fast Pooh.

"He's a menace!" insisted Rabbit.

"Don't be ridickerous!" said Tigger. "The only good Pooh is a fast Pooh!"

At that very moment, Pooh whooshed by, pulling Tigger's stripes off.

"I wish he wouldn't do that," complained Tigger.

Rabbit, Piglet and Tigger went looking for Gopher. After all, this new, improved Pooh was all his idea.

"What'sss everybody complaining about? Pooh'sss perfect! Why, he's the fastessst—"

Before Gopher could finish the sentence, Winnie the Pooh sped by in a cloud of dust. Rabbit wrapped his arms around a mailbox and held on for dear life, and Gopher dug himself a hole in the ground.

When the dust settled, Rabbit went to the edge of the hole and called down.

"Well, Gopher, as you can see, your Perfect Bear isn't so perfect, after all!"

Gopher stuck his head up out of the hole. "You're right about that, sssonny!"

Gopher started thinking. There had to be a way to slow Pooh down, and he would have to find it.

"I've got it!" cried Gopher. He found a large net that would stretch across the path. He and Rabbit held it on one side, while Tigger and Piglet held it on the other.

"This will absssolutely, posssitively ssslow Pooh down!" said Gopher.

Moments later, Pooh flew by in a blur. When he was gone, Rabbit, Tigger and Piglet found themselves knotted up in the net.

Gopher frowned. Slowing down Pooh was going to be a lot harder than he had thought. "Let'sss try Plan Two," said Gopher.

That afternoon, Gopher booby-trapped the bridge at a river crossing.

"How will this slow Pooh down?" asked Piglet.

Gopher explained. "Pooh will cross the bridge, the bridge will fall, Pooh will drop into the water. Sssimple!"

But when Pooh got there, he zoomed across the bridge and nothing happened.

"I don't understand!" cried Gopher, running onto the bridge. Suddenly, the bridge gave way. Gopher splashed down into the river.

"Pooh asked for it!" said a soggy Gopher. "Now he'sss going to get Plan Three!"

Gopher blew up a giant balloon and pressed it between two trees. Rabbit, Tigger and Piglet stood by, watching.

"There!" said Gopher, smiling. "Sssoon as he hitsss thisss, he'll—"

But Gopher never finished speaking. Pooh whizzed by and sped right through the balloon, leaving it perfectly intact.

Gopher shook his head in frustration.

"There's jussst no sssslowing that bear down!"

Gopher was right. Pooh was picking up speed as he went. In no time he had crashed into Eeyore.

"Sorry," said Pooh. "I'm trying not to be late."

"Don't see why. Sooner you get to a place, the sooner somebody asks you to leave," said Eeyore.

"Perhaps I should ask the others what I'm late for."
"Mind if I tag along?" asked Eeyore.
"What a good idea!" said Pooh, and off they went.

Meanwhile, Gopher was telling his friends about a new solution to the problem of Pooh. "There's only one thing to do," said Gopher, "and that'sss ressstore the balance."

"Restore the what?" asked Piglet, confused.

"The balance! The natural order of thingsss! Get thingsss back the way they were!" said Gopher.

Rabbit wondered how Gopher planned to do that.

"Easy!" Gopher explained. "We can't ssslow Pooh down, so we'll ssspeed up!"

The next day, Rabbit raced through his garden, pulling up ripe turnips and planting new seeds.

Meanwhile, Piglet was busy scrubbing clothes at lightning speed.

As for Gopher, he dug tunnels through the ground in record time.

Even Tigger speeded up, bouncing faster than ever.

Tigger bounced right by Pooh and Eeyore without noticing them.

"Uh, Tigger?" Pooh called after him. But Tigger didn't hear him.

Pooh shrugged his shoulders, looking at Eeyore. "I know I'm late for something," said Pooh. "If I don't remember what it is, I shall very likely be late for being late!"

While Pooh and Eeyore tried to figure out what Pooh was late for, Rabbit collapsed on the ground nearby.

"Don't know how much longer I can keep up this pace," said Rabbit.

"Er…Rabbit," said Pooh.

But Rabbit was too exhausted to notice Pooh.

Piglet wandered up on wobbly legs and fell against Rabbit.

"I'm afraid Very Small Animals such as myself get tired rather quickly," said Piglet, panting.

"Excuse me, Piglet," said Pooh. But Piglet was too pooped to notice Pooh, though he was standing close by.

Next, Gopher stuck his head up out of a new tunnel alongside Rabbit and Piglet. He crawled out of the hole, breathing heavily.

"Can't tunnel another inch at this speed," he said, gasping.

Soon, Tigger joined them. "I don't think I can bounce another bounce," said Tigger, fainting.

All the while, Pooh and Eeyore stood there wondering what was going on.

"I think I've missed something very important," Pooh whispered to Eeyore. Then he turned to his tired friends.

"Hello, everyone. I'm sorry for being late."

"But you're not late for anything, Pooh," said Rabbit, thinking he was talking to the new, faster Pooh.

Pooh shook his head sadly.

"It was bound to happen," said Pooh, sighing. "I'm always late for something. Now I'm late for nothing."

Rabbit finally realized that the old Pooh, the slow Pooh, was there right beside him.

"Why, Pooh! It's you! The old, slow you!"

The others got up, excited.

"It worked!" cried Gopher. "The balance is ressstored! We don't have to hurry anymore!"